S0-AND-656

This book belongs to: Pip
and to: Timothy Vanderlong
and to:...
....
....
....

FSC
www.fsc.org

MIX
Paper from
responsible sources
FSC® C118365

Copyright © 2022 Clavis Publishing Inc., New York

Originally published as *Het boek van Pip* in Belgium and the Netherlands by Clavis Uitgeverij, 2022
English translation from the Dutch by Clavis Publishing Inc., New York

Visit us on the Web at www.clavis-publishing.com.

No part of this publication may be reproduced or stored in a retrieval system,
or transmitted in any form or by any means, electronic, mechanical, photocopying,
recording, or otherwise, without the prior written permission of the publisher,
except in the case of brief quotations embodied in critical articles and reviews.
For information regarding permissions, write to Clavis Publishing, info-US@clavisbooks.com.

Pip's Book written and illustrated by Guido Van Genechten

ISBN 978-1-60537-789-6

This book was printed in August 2022 at Nikara, M. R. Štefánika 858/25, 963 01 Krupina, Slovakia.

First Edition
10 9 8 7 6 5 4 3 2 1

Clavis Publishing supports the First Amendment and celebrates the right to read.

Guido Van Genechten

Pip's Book

peep peep peep peep
peep

Clavis
NEW YORK

Welcome!
I'm so happy you're here.
My name is Pip and this is my book.

Woof
Woof
Woof
Woof
Woof
Woof

Hold on . . .

. . . I hear someone else.
Ah, my friend Timothy Vanderlong.
Timothy is the longest dog in the world.
Would you like to see Timothy?

All right, I'll call for him.
Do you want to join me?

Go ahead.

ong!

Timothy!
Timothy Vanderlong!

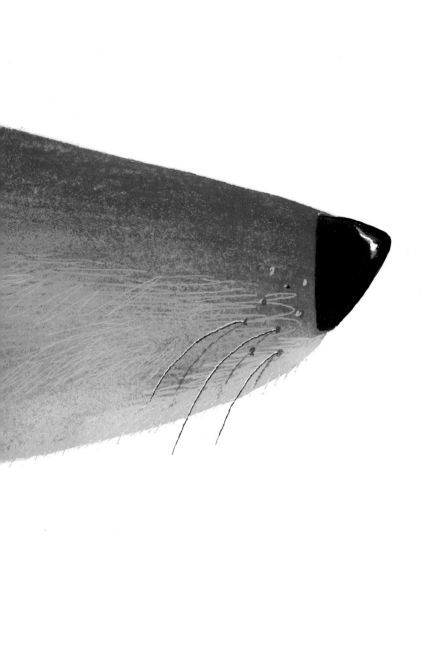

Look, there he is!
Come on, Timothy.
Come on, boy.

He's a little shy.

Let's pet his nose gently.
I'm sure he'll come closer.

There you go, boy.

Come on.

There's room for you.

A little further, Timothy.

We'd really like to see ALL of you, Timothy.

Just a little more, a tad more,
a teeny-tiny bit more and . . . STOP!

Sorry, boy, but we can't see your behind.
Can you walk a little further?
Further, further, a bit further and . . .

Uh . . . no, that's not what I meant.

You can stand on four legs again.
And then tuck up your tummy. Look.

No, that's not going to work either.
Relax your tummy
before you break in half.

Maybe you can lie on your back?
With your head a bit like this?
And that part a little that way?
Go ahead and try.

Well done,
Timothy.
We're almost there.
Now those two
paws up there.
And your tail.

Wow, so much space!

From now on, it's OUR book, Timothy.

Thank you, Pippy.
I feel com-plete-ly
like myself again.

Do you think there's still
some space in OUR book
for my friend Elly?

**p! Pippy!
This is never going to work.
I don't fit inside your book. I'm sorry.**

But, Timothy, it **has** to work.
Wait . . . I know what to do! Of course.
My book needs to be BIGGER!

Help me pull, boy.
Over here.

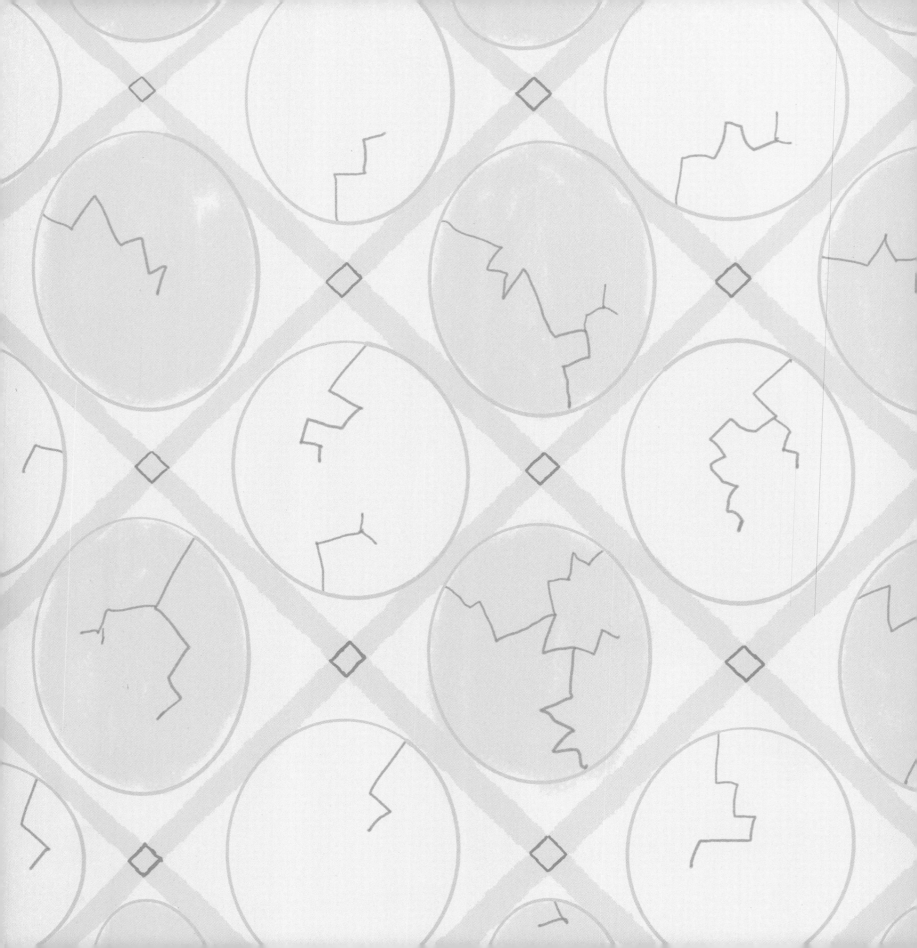